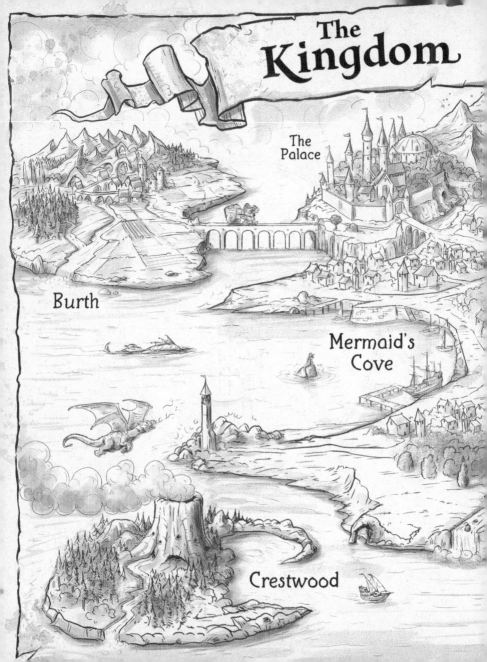

The Kingdom of Wrenly

4

The Witch's Curse

By Jordan Quinn

Illustrated by Robert McPhillips

LITTLE SIMON

New York   London   Toronto   Sydney   New Delhi

LITTLE SIMON

An imprint of Simon & Schuster Children's Publishing Division

1230 Avenue of the Americas, New York, New York 10020

First Little Simon edition August 2014

Copyright © 2014 by Simon & Schuster, Inc.

For information about special discounts for bulk purchases, please contact Simon & Schuster Special Sales at 1-866-506-1949 or business@simonandschuster.com.

The Simon & Schuster Speakers Bureau can bring authors to your live event. For more information or to book an event contact the Simon & Schuster Speakers Bureau at 1-866-248-3049 or visit our website at www.simonspeakers.com.

Manufactured in the United States of America 0419 MTN

8 10 9

Library of Congress Cataloging-in-Publication Data

Quinn, Jordan.

The witch's curse / by Jordan Quinn ; illustrated by Robert McPhillips.

pages cm. — (The kingdom of Wrenly ; 4)

Summary: "It's been raining nonstop for six whole days. Someone has cursed the kingdom of Wrenly! Can Lucas and Clara figure out who's behind the evil spell and stop the villain before it's too late?"

— Provided by publisher.

ISBN 978-1-4814-0075-6 (pbk) — ISBN 978-1-4814-0076-3 (hc) —
ISBN 978-1-4814-0077-0 (eBook) [1. Princes—Fiction.
2. Friendship—Fiction. 3. Rain and rainfall—Fiction. 4. Blessing and cursing—Fiction. 5. Magic—Fiction.] I. McPhillips, Robert, illustrator.
II. Title.

PZ7.Q31945Wi 2014

[Fic]—dc23

2013028259

CONTENTS

CHAPTER 1

Rain, Rain, Go Away!

Heavy rain pelted the windows in Prince Lucas's turret bedroom. It had rained for six days, and Lucas had grown bored. He had read every book he owned. He had played at least a hundred games of checkers and backgammon. He had draped blankets over the tables in the playroom and called it Fort Wrenly. He even taught Ruskin, his pet scarlet

dragon, a few new tricks.

Is this rain ever going to stop? Lucas wondered. He looked out the window and sighed. Ruskin sighed too. If Lucas was bored, Ruskin was bored.

The storm had been fun at first.
Lucas and his best friend, Clara,
had made a mud slide on the hill
behind the castle. They'd slid down
the hill until the grass had worn off.
They'd swooshed down the muddy

slide again and again, tearing holes in their trousers and bloomers.

"Wash up!" Clara's mother, Anna Gills, had cried as she tossed two bars of soap out the back door. "No tracking mud into the castle!"

Lucas and Clara had each picked up a bar and squeezed it. The soap shot out of their fists and landed in a puddle. They'd squealed with laughter. Then they'd rubbed the soap on their hair and clothes and rinsed off in the rain.

But day after day the rain kept coming. Water rushed down the main road like a river. Some of the villagers' homes had flooded. Others had leaky roofs. Clara hadn't come over to play in days.

Queen Tasha and King Caleb had grown worried about all the rain. They were talking about it when Lucas and Ruskin entered the throne room.

"I've never seen so much water," the queen declared.

"We haven't had this much rain in one year, let alone in one summer," said the king. "The farmers will lose their crops if it doesn't stop."

"Does that mean we'll run out of food?" asked Lucas.

"Of course not," said the king, though he wasn't really sure. He ran his hand over his blond hair. "Something's not right."

"Maybe it's a spell," Lucas said.

No sooner had he spoken those words than lightning cracked, and *ka-boom!*—thunder rattled the castle windows. Ruskin yelped and hid under the king's throne.

"Perhaps you're right," the king said as he stroked his chin thoughtfully. "But who would do such a thing?"

CHAPTER 2

The Witch of Bogburp

The royal trumpets trilled. The king and queen looked at each other in surprise.

"Who could be at the door on a day like this?" questioned the king.

Stefan, one of the king's men, entered the throne room.

"Your Majesty, the Witch of Bogburp wishes to see you," he said as he bowed slightly.

The king frowned. He hadn't seen the Witch of Bogburp in years, and for good reason. She used to be the king's adviser, and although she had meant well, she had made a lot of terrible mistakes. One time the witch had offered to make the king's apples the sweetest in the entire

kingdom. The king loved apples and gave his permission. The witch sprinkled magical plant food on the trees, but instead of making delicious apples, the trees withered and died.

Another time the king had wanted a sweet, cuddly kitten. The witch brought him a beautiful white kitten with golden eyes. The cat hissed and spat whenever it saw the king. To make matters worse, it disobeyed all the rules. The king named the cat Mischief because she always got into trouble. She knocked over the queen's perfume collection and smashed all the bottles. Then she fell down the garderobe—the palace toilet—and was flushed into the moat. Stefan had to fish her out and give her a bath.

If that wasn't enough, the witch had given the king a special blond tonic to cover a few gray hairs. But instead of covering the gray, it had made his hair fall out! Luckily, the king's hair had grown back, but his friendship with the witch had not. She was no longer welcome at the

castle, nor anywhere else on the castle grounds. She had been banished to her tree house in Bogburp. Yet here she was, knocking at the door.

The king was about to send the witch away when the queen said, "Perhaps she's changed, Caleb. Let's hear what she has to say."

The king sighed.

"Very well," he said. "Send her in."

Stefan presented the Witch of Bogburp to the king and queen.

Ruskin took one look at the witch and scampered behind Lucas. Lucas remembered her slightly from the

days when she had worked at the palace.

The witch had a short, stubby body, a large hooked nose, and elfish ears. She wore a black cloak and had wet pointy leather shoes on her feet. A bonnet with a tail and a tassel sat on top of her scraggly black hair, and where her right eye should have been, the witch had a glass eye. Sometimes it rolled around in the socket when she spoke. Lucas could never quite

tell where she was looking. It made him uneasy. To top it off, she had a black raven perched on top of her walking stick. "What brings you to the castle, Tilda?" asked the king in a calm, but not-so-friendly tone.

The Witch of Bogburp smiled,

revealing a missing tooth on one side. She bowed slightly.

"I have come to mend my ways, Your Majesty."

CHAPTER 3

A Price to Pay

"And how do you plan to mend your ways?" asked the king.

A crooked smile swept over the witch's face as lightning flashed outside the throne room windows.

"Why, I can put an end to all this rain," she said sweetly.

Thunder boomed and rumbled around the castle.

King Caleb looked at the witch

suspiciously. "And what do you know about the rain?" he asked.

"I know it's a curse," said the witch.

The king leaned back in his throne. "And what do you want to do about it?" he asked.

The witch's glass eye bulged in its socket. "I don't *want* to do anything," she said. "I like the rain. But if never-ending rain isn't good for your kingdom, I may be able to help."

The king desperately needed help. He had no idea how to stop the rain, and the witch knew it. He couldn't allow the kingdom's crops to be ruined.

"I suppose I will have to accept your offer," said the king.

"Of course you will," said the witch, who now knew that she, not the king, had the power. "But there will be a small price to pay."

The king gripped the arms of his throne and leaned forward. "And what is your price?"

"I only require three things," said the witch. Then she held up a bony finger for each. "A cauldron made

of gold, your bejeweled family ring with the royal crest, and the queen's diamond-and-emerald scepter."

The king's jaw dropped. "Such a high price!" he cried. "My ring and the queen's scepter are sacred symbols of our right to rule Wrenly. We cannot part with them."

"Very well," said the witch. "Then your kingdom will drown and your people will suffer."

The king hung his head. He knew there was no other way to save his kingdom. He felt helpless.

Then the queen gently laid her hand on her husband's knee. "I will pay the price," she said.

The king looked at his wife. He gained courage from her words.

"And I will give you my ring," said the king.

The witch rubbed her hands together greedily. Ruskin growled, and Lucas pulled him close.

"And what about the golden cauldron?" asked the witch.

"I'll have the goldsmith forge one without delay," said the king. "We'll deliver everything to your home in Bogburp."

The old woman cackled. Her black cloak swirled as she disappeared out the door. Her raven followed behind.

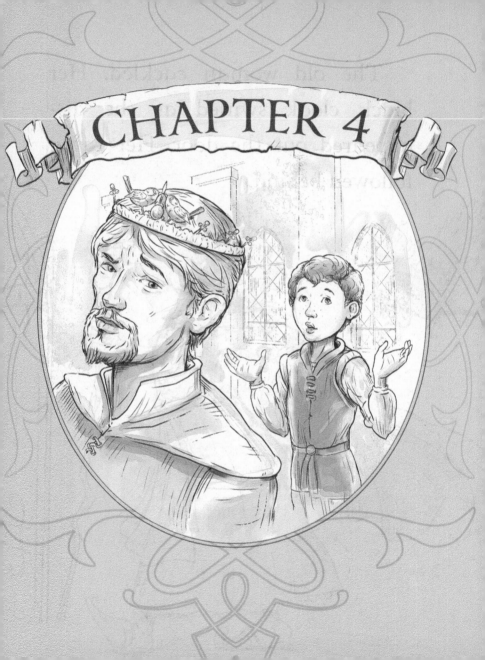

CHAPTER 4

Finger-Pointing

"How could you?" Lucas cried.

"What choice did I have?" asked the king.

"You didn't have to promise your ring and scepter," said Lucas. "We could've found another way."

"Some matters require the help of witches and wizards," the king said.

"And some matters are *caused* by witches and wizards," Lucas argued.

"What are you suggesting?" asked the king.

Lucas put his hands on his hips. "I think I know who's behind the curse," he said.

"You do?" questioned the king. "And who might that be?"

"It's Grom," said Lucas, folding his arms.

The king rolled his eyes. "Why would Grom do such a thing?" he asked.

"Because he's always in a bad mood," said Lucas.

"Not a good reason," said the king.

"And he doesn't have any friends, except his brother,

André," Lucas went on. "And he locks himself in his tower on Hobsgrove all day so no one can see what he's doing."

"Wizards like privacy," said the king.

"I'll bet he wants to take over the kingdom," said Lucas.

"That's ridiculous," the king said.

"Then why did he want Ruskin's shells after he hatched? Everyone

knows scarlet dragon shells have the strongest magical powers in the kingdom."

"He just wanted them for his potions," said the king. "Any wizard would want scarlet dragon shells."

Lucas sighed. "I don't trust him."

"Grom may not be the most fun-loving wizard," said the king, "but he's always done things to help the kingdom."

"And be careful about blaming him for something he may not have

done," added the queen. "You must have all the facts first."

Lucas knew better than to argue with his parents. But he was sure that Grom was behind the curse. *I'll just have to prove it,* he thought. *But I'll need help.*

"Father, may I please go over to Clara's house?" asked Lucas. "I can't stand being cooped up in the castle any longer."

"No," the king said firmly.

"But, Father, it's not very far," Lucas pleaded. "And I'll take Ruskin with me."

"Perhaps it would be a good idea for Lucas to check in on the Gillses,"

said the queen. "I'd like to know how they're faring in the storm."

"May I, Father?" begged Lucas. "Please?"

The king threw his hands in the air. "Now how am I supposed to rule a kingdom when I can't even rule my own family?" he said.

The queen laughed. "We promise to keep that a secret," she said.

Then Lucas grabbed his cloak, and he and Ruskin scampered to the stables.

CHAPTER 5

A Rainy Mission

Lucas saddled his horse, Ivan, and raced through the rushing water to Clara's. Ruskin clung tightly to Ivan's mane. Rain spattered their faces as they galloped along.

Clara's family lived above her father's bakery, the Daily Bread. Lucas pulled back the reins in front of the bakery. Rainwater had almost reached the top of the first step.

Lucas hitched Ivan to a post under the eaves. Then he jangled the bells on the door. Clara's father, Owen Gills, thumped down the stairs and answered the door.

"Lucas!" he cried. "What on earth are you doing out in this weather?"

"I came to see Clara," Lucas said.

"Come in," said Owen.

Clara's family had stayed safe and well in the storm, but they, too, had grown worried.

"If this rain keeps up, the bakery will soon be filled with water," said Anna.

"And if the crops are destroyed, there will be no wheat for our bread," added Owen.

Lucas assured Clara's parents that the king was working on the problem. Then Lucas, Clara, and Ruskin went to Clara's room. Lucas told Clara about the witch's visit, the curse, and the price his parents agreed to pay to undo the curse. He also told Clara that he thought Grom was the one behind it all.

"How can we prove it?" asked Clara.

"We need to talk to the Witch of Bogburp," Lucas said. "She seems to know the most about the curse."

"So what are we waiting for?" said Clara. Then she asked for permission to go out for a quick ride with Lucas.

"Okay, but be back before dark," said Clara's father.

"We will!" promised Clara.

And they headed out on their rainy mission.

CHAPTER 6

Urp!

Lucas, Clara, and Ruskin stopped at the palace stables and quietly saddled Clara's horse, Scallop. Then they galloped toward Bogburp.

Bogburp was a spongy bog made of water and many dead plants, known as peat. Wrenly farmers harvested the peat and a plant called peat moss. The villagers burned peat in their fireplaces to warm their homes. Sometimes they lined their walls with peat moss to keep out the cold. The Witch of Bogburp lived in the middle of the peat bog up in an old, dead oak tree.

Lucas and Clara grazed their horses on a patch of grass, away from the bog. Dragonflies hummed in the air and frogs plopped into the water around them. *Urp!* went the bog. The very bog itself seemed to be alive. Every few moments, it belched, and bubbles rose to the surface. That's how it had come to be known as Bogburp. Ruskin rushed to the water's edge and sniffed at the bubbles.

In the distance Lucas and Clara saw a tree house in the middle of the bog on a tuft of land. Charms and lanterns hung from the bare, twisted branches. Tucked in the branches, on top of a wooden platform, was a house with a thatched roof, along with two smaller huts. A boardwalk

swirled around the trunk of the tree and led up to the house.

"That's the witch's house," said Clara, who always knew where everything was in the kingdom of Wrenly.

"How are we going to get across

the water?" questioned Lucas.

Clara shrugged as she studied the swamp.

Urp! The bog burped again. Ruskin jumped into the bog and landed on a rock. He leaned over and chomped at the bubbles that had come to the surface. The bog burped again. Ruskin hopped to

another rock and tried to eat the
bubbles. Each time the bog belched,
Ruskin jumped to another rock.

"That's how we'll get across!"
Clara exclaimed.

Lucas and Clara hopped from

rock to rock, following Ruskin, until
they got to the little island with the
oak tree. Then they stepped onto the
witch's rickety dock.

"I hope she doesn't put a curse on
us," Clara said.

"Remember when she cursed the wizard Olaf with clumsiness?" asked Lucas.

"Yes," said Clara, "and he tripped and dropped your mother's emerald pendant over the cliff."

"Maybe this isn't such a good idea," Lucas said.

Clara folded her arms. "That old witch wouldn't dare harm the prince of Wrenly."

Then she began to march up the curvy boardwalk in front of her. Lucas and Ruskin followed right

behind. When they got to the top, they knocked on the door and waited. Footsteps clacked across the wooden floor. A small square in the middle of the door unlatched and creaked open. One glass eye and one real eye peered down at the children.

CHAPTER 7

Eggshells

The witch closed the tiny window and opened the door.

"Oh my!" she cried. "What brings you three to Bogburp in all this wet weather? Have you come to deliver my goods?"

A black cat with green eyes and a crooked tail swirled in and out of the folds of the witch's gray dress.

"No," said Lucas, who found it

hard not to stare at the witch's glass eye. "We've come to ask a few questions."

"Well, come in!" said the witch. "I

haven't had any visitors in ages!"

Lucas, Clara, and Ruskin went into the tree house and looked around. Candles flickered and cast shadows on the walls. The furniture had all been made from logs and branches. A fire burned in a small stone fireplace, and a kettle bubbled over the hearth. Dried flowers and charms hung from the beams, as well as a few cobwebs. A broom stood in the corner, along with the witch's walking stick, which had the raven perched on top. When the raven fluffed his wings, Clara jumped.

"Don't worry about Odin," said the witch. "He's quite friendly."

The raven flew from his

perch and landed on the witch's
shoulder. The stick wobbled back
and forth and made a strange
sound, like a waterfall of seeds. Both
Lucas and Clara glanced at it. The
raven cocked an eye toward Ruskin.
Ruskin flicked his tongue.

Lucas held up his hand to Ruskin.
"No!" he said firmly.

Ruskin settled down.

"Good boy."

"Can I get you both a spot of tea?"
asked the witch.

"No, thank you," said Lucas.
"We're here to learn more about the

rain curse. We want to find out who's behind it."

The witch's smile disappeared. Then she waggled a bony finger at the children.

"You children must not get involved in matters of evil," said the witch. "It could put you in great danger."

"Then so be it," said Lucas, who wasn't about to let the witch scare him.

The witch stroked Odin's feathers. "You're a brave boy," she said. "Tell me, do you think you know who did it?"

"Of course I do," said Lucas. "Grom is behind it."

The witch's smile returned. "And what makes you think it's Grom?" she asked.

Lucas folded his arms. "It has something to do with Ruskin's eggshells," he said. "Grom took them after Ruskin hatched."

The witch's eyes widened and her glass eye swirled aimlessly.

"I see you are very clever, Prince

Lucas," she said. "The scarlet dragon eggshells could have something to do with the rain curse."

"You see!" said Lucas, looking at Clara. "It *is* Grom!"

Clara nodded. "Then what do we do now?" she asked.

"There's only one thing to do," the witch said. "You must go to Grom's castle tower and bring me Ruskin's eggshells. Then I will reverse the curse."

"If we get the eggshells," said Lucas, "will you accept them as payment—instead of my family's ring and scepter?"

"Retrieve the eggshells first!" demanded the witch. "Then perhaps I will lower my price."

Then she cackled with delight.

CHAPTER 8

Grom's Workshop

Lucas, Clara, and Ruskin zigzagged across the rocks of the burping bog. Then they jumped into their saddles. Rain poured down as they galloped across the bridge to Primlox. They left the horses in a public stable and boarded a ship to Hobsgrove.

The castle on Hobsgrove had one tower. Steam swirled from a smokestack on the side of it.

"Grom's workshop is up there," Lucas said, pointing.

They hurried toward the tower. Clara tried the latch on the door.

"It's locked," she said.

"No problem," Lucas said. "Watch this."

Lucas clapped his hands twice. Immediately, Ruskin stood on his hind legs and rested his front claws on the door. He lined his mouth up

with the lock. Then he flicked his forked tongue inside the keyhole. The lock clicked and the door swung open.

Ruskin squawked.

"Good boy!" praised Lucas,

patting his dragon on the head.

"What a great trick!" Clara said.

"Thanks," said Lucas. "We've had lots of time to work on it with all this rain."

They crept inside the cold, dimly lit tower and shut the door. Then they walked up the winding stair-case before them. Around and around they went as they climbed the stairs to the top of the tower. The door to the workshop was open. Lucas peeked inside.

"Nobody's here," he whispered.

"*Phew!*" said Clara.

They tiptoed into the musty lab and looked around. A cauldron bubbled over the large stone fireplace. Next to the hearth was a bellows to stoke the fire. A long table with a scale on it stood in the middle

of the room. A fat book lay open to a page titled "Weather Spells." *More proof,* Lucas thought.

Vessels, potion bottles, and flasks lined shelves throughout the room. Torches flamed in their holders, and

some natural light came in through the windows on either side of the room. Ruskin began to sniff around. Lucas pulled open a drawer of a large chest. Clara took a look at the vessels on the table. She found herbs, fish bones, and ground seashells inside them.

Then Ruskin squawked.

"Shhh!" shushed Lucas. "Someone might hear us!"

Ruskin sniffed a ceramic bowl on the table in front of him.

He squawked again.

Lucas shut the drawer and hurried over. "What is it, boy?"

Ruskin nudged the bowl with his nose. Lucas looked inside.

"Clara!" cried Lucas. "Look what Ruskin found!"

Clara hurried across the room and looked in the bowl. "Ruskin's eggshells!" she exclaimed.

"Quick, put them in here," said Lucas, holding out an empty jar.

Suddenly a large shadow loomed over them.

"Put down the magic eggshells!" boomed a voice from the doorway.

CHAPTER 9

Magic Powder

"What are you doing in my work-shop?" shouted Grom as he slammed the door behind him.

Lucas held on tightly to the jar. Ruskin whined and hid behind Lucas. The children backed away and bumped into a chest. Grom pointed a long, skinny finger at Lucas.

"You are trespassing!" he said.

"I demand to know why you're here."

Lucas took a deep breath and stood as tall as he could. Then he pointed a finger right back at Grom.

"It's all your fault!" he cried. "We know you cursed Wrenly with a never-ending rainstorm, and now we have proof."

Grom's jaw dropped in disbelief.

"You think I did *what*?"

"Cursed the land," said Lucas.

"Why on earth do you think I would do such a thing?" Grom asked.

Lucas hadn't expected Grom to be surprised. He had expected him to be furious at being found out. Lucas began to list the reasons why he thought Grom was guilty.

"Well, because you're grumpy all the time," Lucas said. "And you took the magical eggshells. And your spell book is open to a weather page. And not only that, the Witch

of Bogburp thinks you did it too!"

Grom shook his head sadly.

"I have been saving those dragon eggshells for a rainy day," he said as he looked out the window and watched the rain drip down the glass. Then he looked back at the

children. "My brother, André, and I have served the king in good faith for many years," he said. "We have given him our very best." Grom slumped.

Lucas suddenly began to feel sorry for blaming the curse on Grom. "What's wrong?" he asked.

"I'm sorry you think I would do

such a terrible thing," Grom said, looking down at the floor.

Before Lucas could say anything, Grom grabbed the dragon eggshells and crushed them into a fine powder. He scooped the powder into a small glass jar and handed it to Lucas.

"Do you know what the eggshells of a scarlet dragon can do?"

Lucas and Clara shook their heads.

"They have the power to still a storm," said Grom.

Lucas looked at the powder. Now he didn't know who to believe.

"Then who cursed the kingdom?" he asked.

Grom ran his hand over his beard. "When you visited the Witch of Bogburp, did you see anything unusual in her house?"

"Not really," said Lucas.

"Well, there was something weird about her walking stick," said Clara. "The raven was perched on it, and it made a funny sound when the raven flew away."

"What did it sound like?" Grom asked.

"It sounded like a waterfall of seeds," Clara said.

Grom snapped his fingers.

"That's the sound of a rain stick," he said. "A rain stick has the power to make it rain."

"And that means the witch lied to us," said Lucas.

"Perhaps it's time to teach that miserable witch a lesson," said Grom.

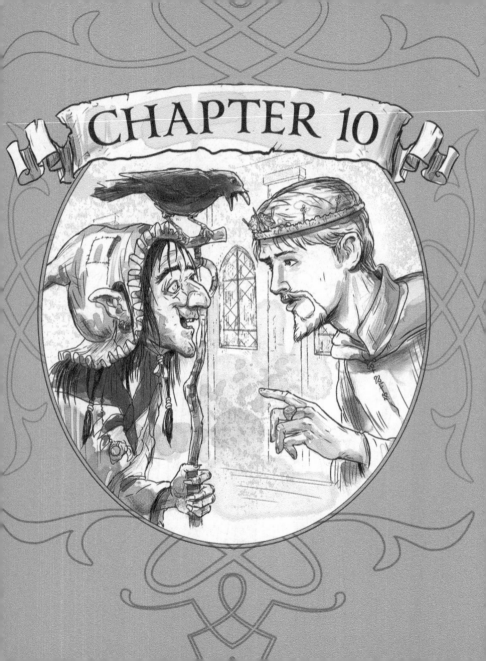

CHAPTER 10

Today's Weather

The next day the king summoned the witch to the palace.

"What's all the fuss about, Your Majesty?" asked the witch.

"Allow me to examine your walking stick," the king said sternly.

"But, Your Majesty, I need the stick to stand up," the witch said.

"Grom, please give Tilda a helping hand," said King Caleb.

Grom held the witch by the arm and loosened her grasp on the walking stick. Odin flew from the stick and onto the witch's shoulder. Then Grom handed the walking stick to

the king. The king
turned the stick
upside down. It
made the sound
of falling seeds.

"Grom tells
me this is a
rain stick," said the king.

"That's ridiculous," said the witch.
"It's nothing more than a cane to
lean on and a perch for my raven."

King Caleb snapped his fingers.

Lucas walked to an open window and shook the scarlet dragon
eggshell powder into the air. The

rain stopped and the clouds began to roll back. Rays of sunshine broke through the clouds, and a rainbow arched over the kingdom. Then the king turned his attention back to the witch and narrowed his eyes.

"Why did you do such wickedness?" he asked.

The witch's shoulders slumped.

"I was going to make the rain stop eventually," she said, "but I liked all the attention."

"Why did you do it in the first place?" asked the king.

The witch sighed. "If I made it

look like I stopped the rain, then you would have thought of me as a hero," she said. "And then you would have welcomed me back to the castle."

"What a crazy idea!" said the

king. "And you would've gotten our riches in the process!"

The witch crumpled to her knees. "I'm sorry," she said as tears welled in her eyes. "I got a bit carried away. It's just that I get so lonely and bored in the bog."

"You will be punished," said the king.

"Yes, Your Majesty," the witch said, wiping a tear off her face.

"You must help the farmers save their crops," said the king. "If you do well, I will see about a better job for you."

The witch smiled slightly. "At least now I'll have a reason to leave my tree house."

Then Lucas raised his hand.

"Yes?" said the king.

"I'd like to apologize," he said.

The king nodded.

Lucas turned toward Grom. "I'm sorry I blamed you for something when I didn't have any proof."

Grom smiled. "All is forgiven, Your Grace."

"Thank you, Grom," said Lucas. Then Ruskin squawked.

"And what did *you* learn, Ruskin?" asked the king.

Ruskin scampered to a nearby door and flicked open the lock with his forked tongue. The door swung open.

"My goodness," said the king.

Then everyone clapped and cheered.

Hear ye! Hear ye!
Presenting the next book from
The Kingdom of Wrenly!
Here's a sneak peek!

"Son," began King Caleb.

Lucas hated it when his father began with the word "son." It rarely ended well.

"This time, you and your mischievous dragon have gone too far," said the king. "You have destroyed Cook's ice and possibly all the food in the larder. Tell me, how could you be so thoughtless?"

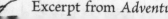

Excerpt from *Adventures in Flatfrost*

Lucas looked at his boots.

"It has become clear that the castle is no place for a dragon," the king went on. "I never should have allowed it."

King Caleb then looked to Queen Tasha for support. The queen nodded for him to go on.

"You have given me no choice," said the king. "Ruskin will have to return to Crestwood for proper training."

Lucas lifted his head and stared at his father in disbelief.

"No, Father! Please don't take

Ruskin away!" he cried. "I promise I'll be better about training him."

The king's face did not soften. "I'm afraid you are *both* in need of training," he declared. "As punishment for your reckless behavior, you and Ruskin will go to Flatfrost first thing in the morning."

"Flatfrost!" cried Lucas. "But why?"

"I want you to apologize to the giants," said the king.

"For what?" questioned Lucas.

"You have caused them more work," said the king. "Therefore you will apologize, and you will also help harvest more ice for Cook."

"But, Father!" protested Lucas.

"No buts," said the king. "You must learn to fix your own mistakes. And when you return, Ruskin will go to Crestwood for training."

Lucas frowned at his father. Then he ran to his room and slammed his door as hard as he could.

Excerpt from *Adventures in Flatfrost*